THE **LION** IN YOUR **HEART**

R.C. CHIZHOV Illustrated by **ANIL YAP**

First published in 2021

Written by R.C. Chizhov
Illustrated by Anil Yap
Interior page design by Bryony van der Merwe

ISBN: 978-1-7379526-0-2 (paperback)
ISBN: 978-1-7379526-2-6 (hardcover)

Published by:
Blissful Conch LLC

Visit us on the web:
thelioninyourheart.com | rcchizhov.com

TO MAX,

who moved homes and
conquered his fear.

Dennis had moved to a new home with Mommy and Daddy.

That night, Dennis lay
WIDE AWAKE
in his bed, too scared to sleep alone in his new room.

"MOMMY, MOMMY!"

he cried.

"What's wrong?" asked Mommy, coming into his room.

"There's a shadow by the window, and I think it's an

O...O...OWL!"

"An owl? Let me look. Oh, it's just the curtain swaying in the wind. See?"

Mommy tied the curtains, tucked Dennis back in bed and kissed him goodnight.

TO DO LIST:
☑ morning class
☑ book reading
☑ homework
☑ teeth

"SWEET DREAMS,
little guy.

I'll leave the nightlight on for you."

Dennis tossed and turned in bed. "Mommy! I CAN'T sleep. I'm still scared."

Mommy returned, "Hmm, I see. It's a new room, and you aren't used to it. But what if I tell you there's a lion in this room?

A FRIENDLY AND DEPENDABLE LION, ALWAYS THERE TO PROTECT YOU."

"A LION?"

Dennis's eyes grew bigger. "But where?"

"Right here, in this room," said Mommy. "Shall we find it?"

Dennis loved finding things.

"Is it under my bed?" he asked.

"No," grinned Mommy.

Dennis tiptoed towards his closet.

"Is it in my clothes?"

"No."

Dennis rummaged through his toys. "Is it in my toy bin?"

Mommy shook her head.

"It's right here, **INSIDE YOU,**" she said, pointing towards his heart.

"Here? But I can't see it."

"True, but you can

FEEL IT.

And you can wake the lion whenever you're scared."

"But how?"

"It's easy, just think of what the lion would do.

What *would* he do if he were scared of sleeping alone at night?"

"The lion would let out a thunderous **ROAAAR!**

Lions are strong and brave. They are not afraid of anything, Mommy! They are the kings of the jungle!"

"Exactly! There will be times when you are frightened or nervous.

But if you wake the sleeping lion in your heart, your

FEAR
WILL
SLOWLY
DISAPPEAR."

Dennis was confused and curious.

"Is the lion in my heart all the time, everywhere I go?"

"Yes, **ALWAYS AND EVERYWHERE.**"

"When I'm doing a
SHOW AND TELL AT SCHOOL
and everyone is watching me?"

"Yes,
BELIEVE IN
YOUR MAGIC,
just like the lion does."

"When I'm surfing in the ocean and
A **BIG** WAVE
COMES MY WAY?"

"Yes, you may be smaller
than the wave, but
YOUR COURAGE IS
BIGGER."

"Will the lion go with me in space,
WHEN I'M ORBITING
Jupiter and Saturn?"

"Yes, he'll be at your side as you

REACH FOR THE STARS."

"Mommy, is there a lion in your heart too?"

"Yes. When I see a
SCARY SPIDER
with eight long legs,

or look down from the
50TH FLOOR
of a tall building,

or have to speak in front of
A HUNDRED
people (gulp!), I breathe in
courage from the lion in my
heart."

Dennis put one hand on his heart and felt his lion beating fast.

"Oh, it's late and way past your bedtime!" said Mommy, glancing at her watch. "Remember, lions need rest and love to sleep."

Dennis rubbed his sleepy eyes and put his head on the pillow. Sleep came quickly.

He dreamed of sitting with his lion and blowing away bubbles of fear together.

He realized that there is

A LION IN EVERYONE.

The lion in **ME** is the lion in **YOU,**

and it's the lion in **ALL OF US.**

THE END